This book belongs to

_____

DISNEY'S
ATLANTIS
THE LOST EMPIRE

A READ-ALOUD STORYBOOK

Adapted by Catherine Hapka
Illustrated by the Disney Storybook Artists
at Global Art Development

Random House New York

Copyright © 2001 by Disney Enterprises, Inc. All rights reserved under International and Pan-American Copyright Conventions. Published in the United States by Random House, Inc., New York, and simultaneously in Canada by Random House of Canada Limited, Toronto, in conjunction with Disney Enterprises, Inc. RANDOM HOUSE and colophon are registered trademarks of Random House, Inc. Library of Congress Card Catalog Number: 00-108354 ISBN: 0-7364-1084-8

Printed in the United States of America
May 2001
10 9 8 7 6 5 4 3 2 1

www.randomhouse.com/kids/disney
www.disneybooks.com

The Search for Atlantis

Atlantis was in danger. A tidal wave was about to crush the city!

The huge crystal called the Heart of Atlantis took the queen as a sacrifice. The Crystal then formed a shield around the city. Atlantis was saved. But the city sank deep below the sea.

Thousands of years later, a scholar named Milo Thatch dreamed of finding the lost city of Atlantis. He knew that a legendary book, *The Shepherd's Journal*, could lead him to the city. But no one else believed that the book—or Atlantis—existed.

Just when Milo was losing hope, a mysterious woman named Helga came to his apartment.

Helga took Milo to meet her boss, Preston Whitmore, a self-made billionaire. Whitmore gave Milo a book. "It's *The Shepherd's Journal*!" Milo cried.

Whitmore then asked Milo to join a team that was searching for Atlantis. Milo's job was to translate the maps and directions in *The Shepherd's Journal*.

"Atlantis is waiting," Whitmore told him. "What do you say?"

Milo was excited to meet the rest of Whitmore's team. There were Commander Rourke and his second-in-command, Helga; Dr. Sweet;

Molière, the dirt specialist; Audrey, the mechanic; Vinny, the explosives expert; Cookie, the chef; and . . .

. . . Mrs. Packard, the communications expert.

Before long, the team's submarine, the *Ulysses*, dove underwater. The search for Atlantis was on! As they moved deeper into the sea, Mrs. Packard heard a strange sound. The noise grew louder and louder.

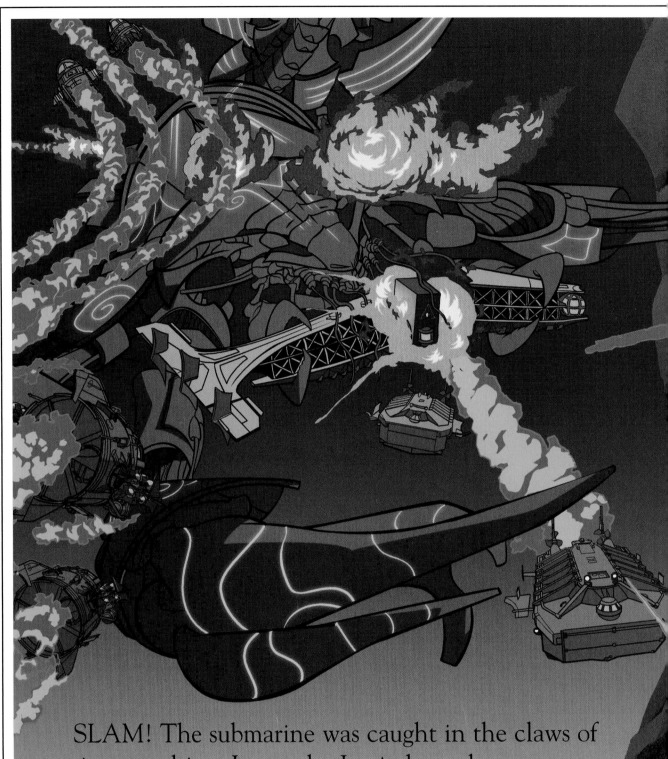

SLAM! The submarine was caught in the claws of a giant machine. It was the Leviathan, the protector of Atlantis!

"All hands abandon ship," said Mrs. Packard. The crew rushed to their escape vehicles.

After a narrow escape, the crew landed in a huge underwater air pocket. Luckily, Milo still had *The Shepherd's Journal*.

"Looks like all our chances for survival rest with you, Mr. Thatch," Rourke said. "You and that little book."

There was a lot of work to do. Milo read
The Shepherd's Journal day and night. Vinny made
a bridge. Audrey fixed the vehicles. Molière plowed
through obstacles.

As they worked together, Milo got to know the other explorers better. They had traveled all over the world looking for adventure and treasure.

One night, after everyone else was asleep, Milo saw some strange fireflies. When they landed, they burst into flames. Soon all the tents were on fire!

19

The explorers jumped into their vehicles and tried to escape over a bridge. But one of the fuel trucks caught fire and exploded. The bridge collapsed.

The vehicles slid backward—down, down, down into a dark cave.

Into the Depths

As Rourke tried to help find his team, Molière examined the dirt. "We are standing at the base of a dormant volcano!" he announced.

Rourke wanted to ask Milo how they should escape. But Milo was missing!

Milo had landed in a different part of the cave—and he was hurt. He woke up to find a band of warriors standing over him. One of the warriors held a crystal against Milo's wounded shoulder. It healed instantly!

Before Milo could thank the strangers, they ran off. He chased them over a crest—and gasped at the sight before him. When the other explorers caught up with him, they saw the city of Atlantis spread out in front of them.

"It's beautiful," whispered Audrey.

The warriors appeared again.

"Welcome to the city of Atlantis," said one of the warriors—who turned out to be a princess named Kida!

Kida led the explorers across an ancient bridge and into the city of Atlantis.

Kida brought Milo, Rourke, and Helga to meet her father, the king.

The king, who was very old and sick, was not happy to see the strangers. He wanted them to leave Atlantis right away.

Rourke asked if they could stay one night. "That would give us time to rest, resupply, and be ready to travel by morning," he said. The king reluctantly agreed.

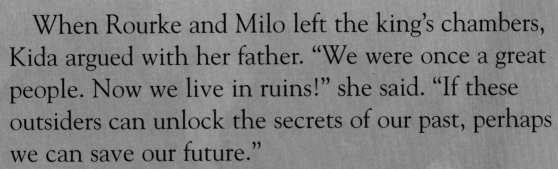

When Rourke and Milo left the king's chambers, Kida argued with her father. "We were once a great people. Now we live in ruins!" she said. "If these outsiders can unlock the secrets of our past, perhaps we can save our future."

But the king did not trust the strangers.

Later that evening, Milo met with Kida. He showed her *The Shepherd's Journal*.

"You can understand this?" Kida asked, staring at the pages. She was shocked. None of her people could read the Atlantean language.

Now Kida had found someone who could help her. She showed Milo a vehicle shaped like a fish. "No matter what I try, it will not respond," she said.

Milo read the words carved into the side of the fish and followed the instructions. Soon the fish was flying around the room!

Kida had more to show Milo. She wanted him to see that Atlantis had once been a great civilization. She showed him all of the city.

Then they swam to some underwater ruins where murals and writings on the walls told the history of Atlantis.

As Milo read, he learned that the city's energy came from a huge crystal—the Heart of Atlantis. Power flowed from the Mother Crystal to the smaller ones the Atlanteans wore around their necks. "It's what's keeping all of Atlantis alive!" Milo told Kida.

"Where is it now?" asked Kida.

"I don't know," Milo replied. That was when he realized that *The Shepherd's Journal* must be missing a page!

The Heart of Atlantis

When Milo and Kida emerged after their swim, Rourke was waiting for them. "You led us right to the treasure chest!" Rourke said with a sneer as he held up the missing page from *The Shepherd's Journal*.

Milo realized that Rourke planned to steal the Heart of Atlantis!

Rourke took Kida and the king prisoner. Then he began the search for the precious Crystal.

Milo refused to help. But Rourke soon found a way into the king's secret chamber. He and Helga took Milo and Kida aboard the aquavator, an underwater elevator.

As the group moved down into a cavern beneath the king's chamber, they saw stones carved with the faces of past kings surrounding the Heart of Atlantis.

In times of trouble, the Crystal needed the energy of a royal Atlantean to protect itself and the city. Beams of light began shooting from the Crystal, searching for someone of royal birth.

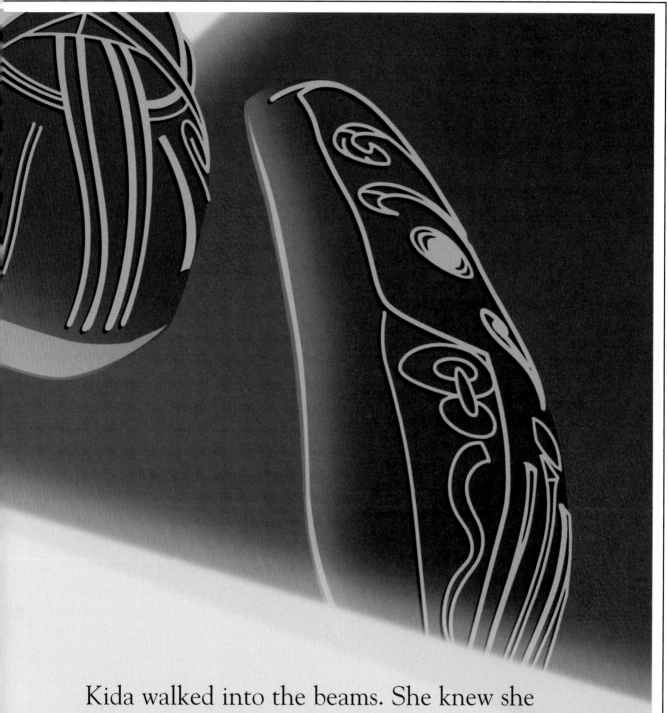

Kida walked into the beams. She knew she
must risk her life to save Atlantis—just as her
mother had done.

"All will be well, Milo Thatch," she said.
She began to crystallize, joining with the
Heart of Atlantis.

Rourke and Helga took the crystallized princess back to the explorers. They told them their plan to take Kida to the surface. Such a large, powerful crystal would be very valuable!

But Cookie, Mrs. Packard, Audrey, Vinny, and Molière refused to help. They decided to stay with Milo and try to save Atlantis.

Dr. Sweet stayed, too. He was helping the king, but it seemed to be too late. The king was dying.

When Milo went to see him, the king handed Milo his crystal and spoke his final words: "Our ancestors left us much wisdom. We must build on their triumphs and learn from their mistakes."

Milo knew he had to save Kida—and Atlantis. But Rourke and Helga were already escaping in a hot-air balloon! They had found a volcano shaft that led to the surface.

Milo showed his friends how to start the fish-shaped vehicles. Soon the entire Atlantean armada took off after Rourke and his troops.

Rourke was desperate to get his balloon up and out of the volcano. To lighten the load, he threw Helga overboard!

In anger, she fired a flare at the balloon, setting it ablaze.

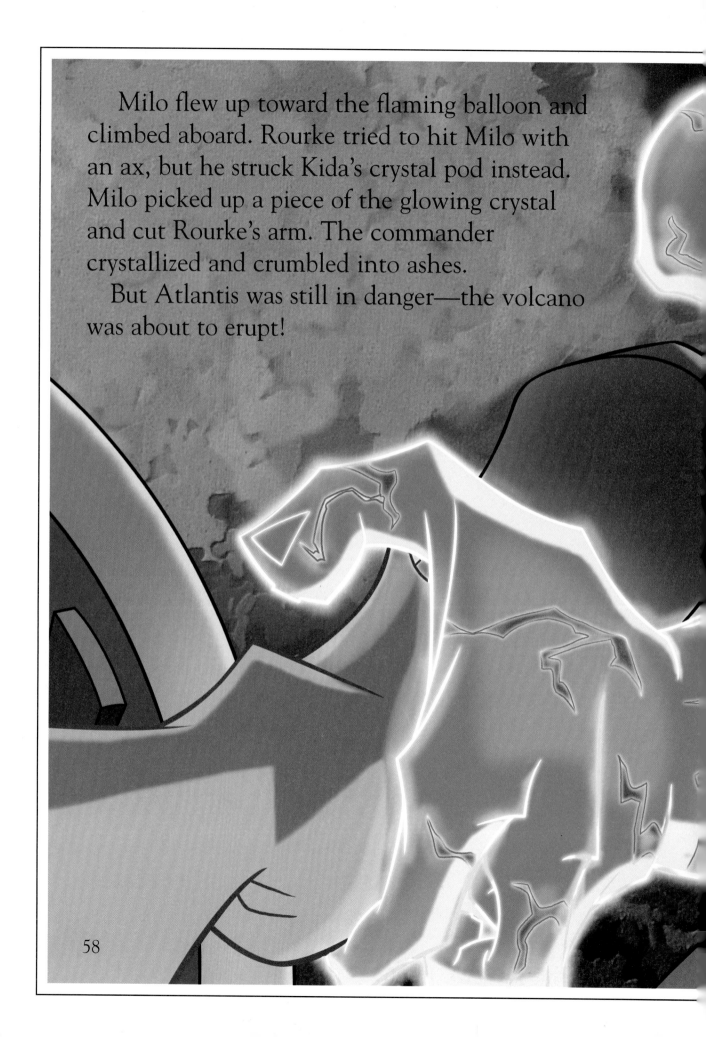

Milo flew up toward the flaming balloon and climbed aboard. Rourke tried to hit Milo with an ax, but he struck Kida's crystal pod instead. Milo picked up a piece of the glowing crystal and cut Rourke's arm. The commander crystallized and crumbled into ashes.

But Atlantis was still in danger—the volcano was about to erupt!

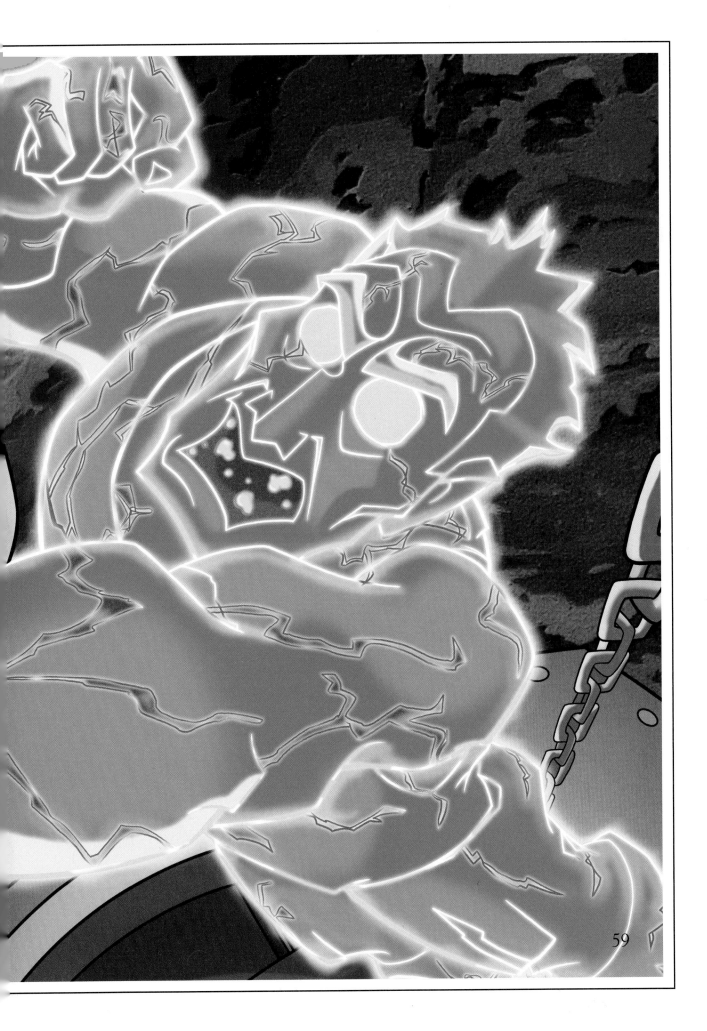

The crystallized princess broke free of her pod and floated above the city. The Stone Giants rose to protect her and the city as the volcano erupted. Atlantis was saved!

Finally, Kida returned to her human form. She floated down into Milo's arms. In the palm of her hand was a bracelet that her mother had taken with her when she was chosen by the Crystal.

After the adventure was over, most of the explorers returned to Mr. Whitmore's mansion. They all agreed to keep Atlantis a secret.

But Milo didn't leave with the rest of the crew. His dream of discovering Atlantis had come true. And now he wanted to stay with Kida in Atlantis forever.